© 1992 The Walt Disney Company

No portion of this book may be reproduced
without the written consent of The Walt Disney Company.

Produced by Kroha Associates, Inc.
Middletown, Connecticut.

Printed in the United States of America.

ISBN 1-56326-123-5

Be Yourself, Daisy!

One crisp Saturday morning in October, Daisy hurried to the bus stop after her piano lesson. She was going to meet Minnie and all her friends at the mall to look for Halloween costumes. When the bus stopped, Daisy got on, but she couldn't see a single empty seat.

"Hi, Daisy!" someone called to her. Daisy looked around. Samantha Hall, an older girl from school, was waving at Daisy. "You can sit next to me if you want," she said.

"Thank you, Samantha," Daisy said as she sat down. She could hardly believe her luck. *Samantha Hall is one of the coolest older girls in school*, Daisy thought. *And she knows my name!*

"Where are you going?" Samantha asked Daisy as the bus started up again.

"To meet my friends at the mall," Daisy explained. "We're looking for costumes to wear to the Halloween carnival and for trick-or-treating."

"I'm going to the mall, too," said Samantha. "But I'm not shopping for a Halloween costume. That's for little kids. I'm buying makeup. Do you want to come with me?"

Daisy was very flattered. "I sure do," she agreed at once.

When they arrived at the mall, Daisy followed Samantha
inside. Minnie, Clarabelle, Lilly, and Penny were waiting for
Daisy at the entrance.

"Hi, Daisy!" Minnie called. "Ready to look for Halloween
costumes?"

"Not today, Minnie," Daisy answered. "I'm going to shop with
Samantha instead. See you later." She strolled off with
Samantha, leaving her friends staring after her in surprise.

"That's not very nice of Daisy," Penny said finally. "We waited
for her, and now she's going off with Samantha."

"Daisy doesn't usually act like that," Lilly added.

"I guess we'll just have to look for our costumes without Daisy," Minnie sighed as she and her other friends went into their favorite store. "It won't be as much fun, though."

Soon the girls were busy looking at costumes.

"We could be clowns," Penny suggested. "I like these funny wigs."

"How about ballerinas?" Clarabelle said, looking at a costume with a pink tutu.

"I know," Minnie said, holding up a bright scarf. "Let's all be gypsies! We can wear big, twirly skirts and lots of scarves and beads!"

"That's a great idea," everyone agreed. They chose colorful scarves, big hoop earrings, and lots of shiny beads and bracelets.

On their way out of the store, the girls saw Samantha and Daisy at the cosmetics counter. Samantha had on red lipstick, and Daisy was putting blusher all over her face with a big fluffy brush.

"Gee, Daisy, you look all set for Halloween!" Penny teased.

"Aren't you kind of young to wear all that stuff?" Clarabelle asked.

"Oh, don't be such babies," Daisy said, frowning. "This makeup makes me look more grown-up!"

On Monday Daisy teetered into the classroom, wearing shoes with high heels instead of her regular play shoes. "How are you going to play tag at recess?" Lilly asked as Daisy wobbled to her desk. "You can't run in those!"

"I don't care if I can run in them or not," Daisy answered. "These shoes are more grown-up, like Samantha's."

Minnie, Clarabelle, Penny, and Lilly just looked at each other and shook their heads.

At lunch, Minnie saved Daisy a place at the cafeteria table. But Daisy walked past to sit with Samantha at the older girls' table.

"Daisy's ignoring us because we're not as old as Samantha," Penny said angrily. "I don't think that's very nice."

"Me either," Minnie sighed. "But I'm not sure there's anything we can do about it."

All that week, Daisy followed Samantha everywhere and did whatever Samantha did. She wore jewelry like Samantha's. She bought a T-shirt just like Samantha's. If Samantha laughed at a joke, so did Daisy. If Samantha went to the arcade after school instead of doing her homework — so did Daisy.

On the morning of the Halloween carnival, Minnie got up early and hurried to Daisy's house to see if she was still coming to the carnival with them. Daisy answered the door in her nightgown.

"Are you sick?" Minnie asked.

"No," Daisy yawned. "Just sleepy. I stayed up really late last night watching scary movies with Samantha and her friends."

"Oh," Minnie said, hesitating. "Well, I came to ask if you're going to the Halloween carnival with us."

"Thanks," Daisy yawned again. "I'm going with Samantha and her friends. But maybe I'll see you there."

Minnie went home, feeling very sad and worried. This would be the first Halloween Minnie could remember when Daisy wouldn't be along to share the fun. Later that day, as she put on her gypsy costume, she thought about how Daisy was acting. Daisy didn't seem to care about her old friends at all.

Soon Clarabelle, Penny, and Lilly arrived at Minnie's house all dressed up in their colorful costumes.

"Is Daisy coming with us?" they asked Minnie.

"No," Minnie sighed. "I guess we'll have to go without her." Everyone was disappointed.

"Well, Daisy's going to miss having a great time," Penny said.

"She sure is, Penny," Minnie agreed. "Now, we promised to be home early, so let's get going!"

Soon the girls were having a wonderful time at the carnival. They rode the Ferris wheel and drove shiny little cars around a track. They ate hot dogs and popcorn. Clarabelle treated everyone to pink cotton candy, and Penny won a stuffed bear by knocking down bottles with a softball.

"Let's ride the carousel next," Minnie suggested to the others. As they ran toward the brightly lit ride, the girls met Daisy and Samantha getting off the roller coaster. Minnie noticed that Daisy was holding her stomach and looked as if she weren't feeling well. "Hi, Daisy," Minnie said. "Do you want to ride the carousel with us?"

But Samantha didn't give Daisy a chance to answer. "Oh, that's for little kids," she said. "The roller coaster is a lot cooler."

"Come on, let's ride it again!" Samantha's friends called as they got back in line.

"Well, okay," Daisy sighed as she trailed after the older girls.

At last it was time to leave. As Minnie and her friends left the carnival, they saw Daisy and Samantha walking by.

"We're leaving now, so we can trick-or-treat and be home before it gets dark," Minnie said to Daisy. "Do you want to come with us?"

"Only babies have to be home before dark," Samantha said. "I'm going in the haunted house. Daisy, are you coming with me or not?" Samantha ran off toward the spooky-looking mansion.

Daisy raced after her. "Wait for me, Samantha!" she called.

But Samantha didn't wait for Daisy. She ran into the haunted house, leaving Daisy all by herself. Daisy took a deep breath and tiptoed through the door. Inside, it was dark and scary and cold.

"Samantha!" Daisy called in a whisper. But no one answered. Daisy's heart pounded as she walked through the dark tunnel. Pictures of witches and goblins grinned down at her. Spooky noises echoed all around her. Sticky spider webs brushed her face. *I know it's just pretend*, Daisy thought, *but I don't like it in here.*

At the haunted house exit, Samantha was waiting for Daisy
with a big grin on her face.

"It wasn't very nice of you not to wait for me," Daisy said.

"So what?" Samantha answered. "You're a big girl."

"Well, I want to go home now, anyway," Daisy replied.

"Go ahead," Samantha answered. "I can stay as late as I want.
If you want to go home, you can go by yourself."

Blinking back tears, Daisy left the carnival. She walked up the
sidewalk as fast as she could, away from the noise and lights of
the carnival. *I wish I had walked home with Minnie,* she
thought. *I wish I hadn't stayed with Samantha. I wish I could
still go trick-or-treating, but now I don't even have a costume.*

Suddenly, Daisy heard a noise around the corner. She stopped and listened. She remembered the scary, late-night movies she'd watched with Samantha and all the spooky things in the haunted house.

"Daisy!" a voice shouted. Daisy shrieked. Then she started to laugh as she saw Minnie, Clarabelle, Penny, and Lilly running toward her.

"Oh, I'm so glad to see all of you!" Daisy exclaimed.

"We were worried about you staying too late," Minnie said. "So we decided to come back and try to find you."

"I'm glad you did!" Daisy exclaimed. "I'm sorry I went to the carnival with Samantha. I didn't have any fun at all!"

"It's not too late to go trick-or-treating with us," Minnie said. "Do you want to come?"

"I wish I could," Daisy said sadly. "But I don't have a costume!"

"Oh, that's no problem!" Minnie said. "You can be a gypsy, too. Here, I'll give you my scarf to wear."

"Take some of my bracelets," Penny offered.

"You can use some of my beads and this fringed shawl," Clarabelle added.

"Carry my tambourine," Lilly said. "And here's an extra treat bag for you from the carnival."

In a few moments, Daisy was a colorful gypsy just like her friends.

"If we hurry, we won't be too late to go trick-or-treating!" Minnie exclaimed. "This is going to be fun!"

"It sure will," Penny agreed. "I love to go trick-or-treating!"

"Me, too," Daisy agreed. "But do you know what's the very best treat?"

"Candy corn!" Clarabelle shouted.

"Bubble gum!" Penny said.

Daisy just shook her head and said, "The best treat of all is being myself — and having friends who like me just the way I am!"

Have you ever tried to act older or different from the way you really are? Write in the enclosed letter and tell me all about it. I promise to answer soon!